SUCH A PRINCE

by Dan Bar-el

Illustrated by John Manders

Clarion Books ♥ New York

Clarion Books
a Houghton Mifflin Company imprint
215 Park Avenue South, New York, NY 10003
Text copyright © 2007 by Dan Bar-el
Illustrations copyright © 2007 by John Manders

The illustrations were executed in gouache and colored pencil.
The text was set in 18-point Centaur.

www.clarionbooks.com

Printed in Malaysia

Library of Congress Cataloging-in-Publication Data

Bar-el, Dan.
Such a prince / by Dan Bar-el ; illustrated by John Manders.
p. cm.
Summary: Libby Gaborchik, a highly unusual fairy, helps Marvin, a poor peasant,
win the hand of the beautiful but love-starved Princess Vera.
ISBN-13: 978-0-618-71468-1
ISBN-10: 0-618-71468-5
[1. Fairy tales. 2. Princesses—Fiction. 3. Humorous stories.]
I. Manders, John, ill. II. Title.
PZ7.B22953Su 2007
[E]—dc22   2006009518

TWP 10 9 8 7 6 5 4 3 2 1

For Bubba
(and all the other
bubbies out there)
—D.B.

For the Princesses
Angelina,
Julia,
and Sonya
—J.M.

Gaborchik is spelled with only one C, but no matter. I don't ask for the fame.

Now, Princess Vera is not dying, and yes, I am a fairy. That's why it takes me only one quick glance to figure out what is the matter with the dear girl. Her problem? Love! The poor thing is starved for love. I mean, aren't we all? But with the young, it's always so dramatic.

"The princess needs to eat three perfect peaches. And she must be married within a week of eating them." That's my advice for the king. Nice and simple. As fairies go, I'm not the flashy kind. Glass slippers and pumpkin carriages are just not my style.

The news spreads throughout the kingdom, and before you know it, there is a line of young men carrying peaches that winds around the castle twice. Peaches in silk bags, peaches in carved boxes, peaches nestled in spun gold. Not perfect peaches, though, the poor darlings.

In one corner of the kingdom is a small cottage where a poor old woman lives with her three sons. The two older sons are big hunks, full of muscle and confidence. The youngest son is . . . well, he's a little on the skinny side. But he has a big heart. The heart is a muscle, too, you know.

Sheldon, the eldest, goes into the orchard out back and picks the three best peaches. He wraps them in a white cloth and says to his mother, "With a little luck, I'll save the princess, marry her, and live the good life forever after."

As Sheldon rides through the dark forest that surrounds the castle, whom should he meet but none other than yours truly, Libby Gaborchik. "What have you got in the cloth, fine sir?" I ask, just to make conversation.

"None of your business, old hag," Sheldon replies rudely. "But if you must know, I have three snakes. Ha!" And off he goes.

"Such a mouth," I think to myself. "If snakes are what you say, then snakes are what you shall have."

Sheldon arrives at the castle and tells the guard that he has three perfect peaches to give to the princess.

"That's all well and good," says the sentry, "but first I must have a peek."

When the cloth is untied, do you think three peaches roll out?

Of course not!
What they find are three
hissing serpents.

Sheldon will not marry the princess and live the good life. What he gets instead is a good beating from the guard and a kick out the castle door.

Sheldon returns home in shame, and so the second eldest son, Harvey, goes into the orchard out back and picks the three next best peaches. He wraps them in a white cloth and says to his mother, "With a little luck, I'll save the princess, marry her, and never work another day in my life."

As Harvey walks through the dark forest, whom should he meet but none other than yours truly, Libby Gaborchik. "What have you got in the cloth, fine sir?" I ask, just because I'm naturally curious.

"None of your business, old hag," he says to me rudely. "But if you must know, I have three toads. Ha!" And off he goes.

"This is the way to talk to a stranger?" I think to myself. "If toads are what you say, then toads are what you shall have."

Harvey arrives at the castle and tells the guard that he has three perfect peaches to give to the princess.

"That's all well and good," says the sentry, "but first I must have a peek."

When the cloth is untied, do you think three peaches roll out?

Of course not!

What they find are three leaping toads. Harvey will not marry the princess and live like a lazy good-for-nothing. What he gets instead is a sound beating from the guard and a kick out the castle door. So Harvey, too, returns home in shame.

Finally, there is Marvin, the youngest. Both his big brothers have come home with nothing to show for themselves, so Marvin thinks, "What do I have to lose?" He goes to the orchard out back and picks three not-so-great peaches and wraps them in a tattered—but clean— kerchief. Then he kisses his mother on the cheek and says, "I'm going to save the princess, marry her, and bring you to live in the castle." His mother smiles and pinches his cheek.

As Marvin walks through the dark forest, whom should he meet but none other than yours truly, Libby Gaborchik. "What have you got in the cloth, fine sir?" I ask, just because I'm a people person.

"I have three perfect peaches for the princess, dear lady," Marvin says to me kindly, "When she eats them, she will get better, and I will marry her, and then I will bring my poor old mother to live with us in the castle."

Such a son. Couldn't you just kiss him? If three perfect peaches are what he wants, then three perfect peaches are what he shall have.

"Listen, Marvin. Before you go, I would like to give you something."

"How did you know my name is Marvin?"

"Oh, a lucky guess. Here, I want you to take this silver whistle. The king has a reputation for making strange requests. Who knows? A whistle might come in handy. At least, darling, it can't hurt."

Marvin makes his way to the castle. He shows the peaches to the guard, who is quite satisfied and wastes no time taking Marvin upstairs to see the royal family.

"Behold, your Majesty! This young man has brought the three most perfect peaches."

Princess Vera eats one peach and lifts her head from the pillow.

She eats the second peach and sits straight up.

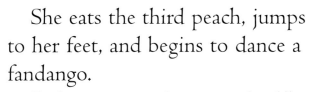

She eats the third peach, jumps to her feet, and begins to dance a fandango.

"This is a good sign, indeed," says the king with a sigh. "You have done us a great service, Marvin."

"Then may I ask for your daughter's hand in marriage?" Marvin asks.

"Oh, yes, Daddy!" Princess Vera shouts, appearing not the least bit sick anymore.

The king takes a long look at poor, skinny Marvin and shudders. Could he let his only daughter marry such a man? He's a pauper, a nobody.

"Well, it's like this, Marvin," he begins. "You did a splendid job with the peaches . . . but there is still one test required of you. Below, in the castle courtyard, are one hundred wild rabbits. The cook is going to make a rabbit stew in celebration of Vera's good health. Tomorrow morning, take them out to graze upon some grass and then bring them back in the evening, nice and plump. You must not lose even one rabbit! Then we'll talk marriage."

The next day, Marvin shoos the rabbits into a field, but he cannot keep them together even for an instant. Such craziness! Rabbits going here. Rabbits going there. Rabbits going everywhere—and then nowhere to be found. Marvin is heartbroken. The sun begins to set, and with it sink his hopes of marriage to Princess Vera.

Ah, but then, darlings, he remembers . . .

Of course, the whistle!

Marvin reaches into his pocket, takes out the silver whistle, and blows once.

Rabbits come out from all directions.

He blows a second time. Rabbits hop into line, one behind the other.

He blows a third time. Rabbits parade over the drawbridge and into the castle.

"... 97, 98, 99, 100. All rabbits accounted for, your Majesty." Marvin beams with pride.

But the king isn't looking so happy. His trick didn't work, and he's beginning to worry. "Er, these rabbits don't look plump enough for a royal stew. Take them out tomorrow for another graze, and then we'll talk marriage."

The next day, the king convinces the queen to dress up as a peasant. She walks into the field where Marvin is watching over the rabbits.

"Excuse me, young man," the queen says. "I am so very hungry. You have so many rabbits. Surely you could spare just one."

"Of course, kind lady. I would not deny a hungry person food."

But then who should walk by but none other than yours truly, Libby Gaborchik, taking a stroll, just to stay active.

"Such a fancy ring she has," I point out quietly to Marvin. "How does a poor peasant manage to afford one, I wonder?"

Marvin is confused for a moment, but then he gets the picture. He holds up a nice fat rabbit and offers it to the woman.

"I will give you this rabbit if you stand on your head for three seconds."

The queen turns as red as a borscht beet, but since she doesn't want to disappoint the king, she performs her half of the bargain. Not a pretty picture, you can be sure. With her legs flailing in the air and her dress over her head . . . I could have gone through life quite happily without such a memory.

The queen takes the rabbit from Marvin and runs back to the castle. The king is delighted, because now the marriage can be called off. Or so he thinks.

Back in the field, the sun is setting, so Marvin blows his whistle once. The rabbit squirms out of the king's hand. Marvin blows the whistle a second time. The rabbit squiggles through the castle gate. Marvin blows the whistle a third time, and the rabbit squeezes into line just in time to join the other rabbits marching over the drawbridge.

"... 97, 98, 99, 100. All rabbits accounted for, your Majesty. Now may I marry Princess Vera?"

"Well, Daddy?" asks Vera, who is beginning to find Marvin very interesting.

"No! . . . I mean, wait." The king tries to remain pleasant. "Let's give these rabbits one more day to fatten up."

The next day, the king disguises himself as a peddler and rides out into the field on an old donkey.

"Excuse me, young man," the king says. "I am so very hungry. You have so many rabbits. Surely you could spare just one."

"Of course, kind sir. I would not deny a hungry person food."

But then who should walk by but none other than yours truly, Libby Gaborchik, taking a stroll, just to stay busy.

"Such fancy boots he has," I point out quietly to Marvin. "How does a poor peddler manage to afford them, I wonder?"

Marvin is confused for a moment, but then he gets the picture. He holds up a nice fat rabbit and offers it to the man.

"I will give you this rabbit if you kiss your donkey three times on the lips."

The king nearly loses his temper. But what can he do? He looks around to make sure no one is watching, then kisses the donkey three times on the lips. After a lot of spitting, the king takes the rabbit, rides back to the castle, locks the kitchen door behind him, and throws the rabbit into a pot on the stove. Marvin will not be his son-in-law, he thinks.

But Marvin is not worried. He takes his whistle and blows once. The rabbit jumps out of the pot. He blows the whistle a second time. The rabbit jumps up onto the high windowsill. He blows the whistle a third time. The rabbit jumps out the window and over the moat, just in time to join the other rabbits marching over the drawbridge.

". . . 97, 98, 99, 100. All rabbits accounted for, your Majesty. Now may I marry Princess Vera?"

"Oh, yes, Daddy!" shouts Vera, without the least bit of modesty.

"Hold your horses, both of you. There is one final test." The king fixes Marvin with a menacing stare. He can see that there is more to this poor peasant than meets the eye. But if he can't outsmart him, perhaps he can still scare him away. "A princess deserves nothing less than an honest man. Are you an honest man?" he growls. "Are you brave enough to declare before my court three truths . . . upon your life?"

"Not a problem, your Majesty," says Marvin.

The palace fills with court officials who have come to witness this last challenge.

Marvin clears his throat. "True or false, did I not bring you three perfect peaches that made Princess Vera well again?"

"Oh, yes, Daddy. He did!" shouts Vera in a most un-princess-like voice.

"First truth, upon my life," says Marvin. "True or false, did not the queen stand on her head for three seconds?"

"True," whispers the queen, wishing she could crawl into a corner.

Murmurs and gasps spread throughout the palace.

"Second truth, upon my life," says Marvin, "And finally, your Majesty, did you not three times kiss your—"

"That's enough truth!" the king quickly interrupts. "More than enough! Test's over. Why waste any more time when two young people are so eager to get married?"

"Oh, yes, Daddy!" shouts Vera, lifting Marvin in her arms.

So what more is there to say? Marvin is now Prince Marvin. His mother is retired and living the good life. Vera is healthy, and the king and queen have less stress. Oh, and I turned Sheldon and Harvey into reptiles.

A joke, darlings, a joke! Libby Gaborchik is just making a small joke. Laughing is good for your health. Trust me, I'm a fairy. I know these things.